Delilah Darling

IS ON T

Jeanne Willis wrote her firs... ...hen she was
five years old and hasn't stopped writing since.
She has now written over a hundred titles, including
picture books, novels and television scripts.
She has won numerous awards, including the
Children's Book Award, the Sheffield Children's
Book Award and the Silver Nestlé Smarties Prize.
Her teen novel, *Naked Without a Hat*, was
shortlisted for the Whitbread Award in 2003.
She writes with her pet rat keeping her company
and often takes inspiration from dreams and
interesting conversations with strangers.

Delilah Darling

IS ON THE STAGE

Jeanne Willis

Illustrated by Rosie Reeve

PUFFIN

PUFFIN BOOKS

Published by the Penguin Group

Penguin Books Ltd, 80 Strand, London WC2R 0RL, England
Penguin Group (USA) Inc., 375 Hudson Street, New York, New York 10014, USA
Penguin Group (Canada), 90 Eglinton Avenue East, Suite 700, Toronto, Ontario, Canada M4P 2Y3
(a division of Pearson Penguin Canada Inc.)
Penguin Ireland, 25 St Stephen's Green, Dublin 2, Ireland (a division of Penguin Books Ltd)
Penguin Group (Australia), 250 Camberwell Road, Camberwell, Victoria 3124, Australia
(a division of Pearson Australia Group Pty Ltd)
Penguin Books India Pvt Ltd, 11 Community Centre, Panchsheel Park, New Delhi – 110 017, India
Penguin Group (NZ), 67 Apollo Drive, Rosedale, North Shore 0632, New Zealand
(a division of Pearson New Zealand Ltd)
Penguin Books (South Africa) (Pty) Ltd, 24 Sturdee Avenue, Rosebank,
Johannesburg 2196, South Africa

Penguin Books Ltd, Registered Offices: 80 Strand, London WC2R 0RL, England

puffinbooks.com

First published 2008
1

Text copyright © Jeanne Willis, 2008
Illustrations and original character copyright © Rosie Reeve, 2008
All rights reserved

British Library Cataloguing in Publication Data
A CIP catalogue record for this book is available from the British Library

ISBN: 978-0-141-32281-0

For Sue Langley, with love from J.W.

To Ella and Nina, from R.R.

Chapter One

In case you don't know, my name is Delilah Darling and I am extremely famous. Actually my whole name is *Queen* Delilah, but you can just call me Delilah if you want. Or Diddles. Or Queenie. In the Far Away Land where I come from, we always call our friends funny names. And our enemies.

I like to call my little brother Smallboy, but my mother says, 'Delilah, darling, his name is James.' But you mustn't take any notice of her. She's got a terrible memory, poor old thing. Next she'll be telling you I'm not really a queen and that I've always lived here with her and Daddy, but that's nonsense, I'm afraid.

I really do come from a land far, far away. I can't tell you its name because it's too hard to say but it's a little island in between Jafrica and Smindia. I think you would like to go there because it is wonderful fun, but I'm afraid I can't show you where it is exactly. This is because somebody forgot to draw it on the map, which was rather silly of them.

Where I come from, if someone
forgets to draw something on a map,
they are thrown to the crocosmiles,
which are a bit like crocodiles only
smilier. And furrier. My Far Away Land
has its own special sort of animals and
its own flowers and sweets and games
and money and everything. It even has
its own language.

Smallboy speaks Far Away Language all the time. Which is why nobody understands a word he says except for me. Even Gigi can't understand him, but that's because she's French. Gigi is our Old Pear, which is someone who tries to look after us while our parents are busy. This isn't an easy job because sometimes Gigi misbehaves.

Like now, she is on the phone to her boyfriend, who is called Etienne. She is going kiss, kiss, kiss and *mwa, mwa, mwa*. Where I come from, we never kiss boyfriends on the telephone. We chase them round and round the playground until they are worn out. Then we catch them and stuff grass up their jumpers. Or crispy leaves, if it's autumn.

Gigi is not supposed to be talking to Etienne on the telephone. She is supposed to be helping me read my school play. Of course, I can read all by myself in the land where I come from. I can even read long words like

Rhinoceroo and Smelliphant and Hippobottymus. The only reason I can't read the words in this play is because my eyes are shut.

My school play is called *The Gingerbread Man*. I think it's about a man made out of gingerbread, but I'm not sure because I wasn't listening very much. The reason I wasn't listening is this:

When my teacher Mrs Mullet was reading us the play during Story Time, my best boyfriend Lucian Lovejoy kept making a funny buzzing noise in his trousers. I asked if he had a pet wasp and Horrid Charlotte Griggs heard me and she put her hand up and shouted, 'I'm telling! Mrs Mullet? Mrs Mu–llet! Lucian Lovejoy is playing with wasps again.'

Which was a horrid thing to say. Where I come from, nobody ever tells the teacher if someone is playing with something they shouldn't. Anyway, it wasn't even a wasp. It was a rubber band wrapped round and round and round a bubblegum wrapper, which went *buzz* and *pthhhh* when Lucian let go of it. Only, Mrs Mullet didn't know that, so she made him come to the front of the reading rug to check his pockets and that is when he gave me the buzzy thing to hide. So I sat on it.

I did try really, really hard to listen to the story of the gingerbread man, but I had to keep testing Lucian Lovejoy's buzzy thing to make sure it still worked. Then, right in the middle of telling the story, Mrs Mullet snapped the book shut and went huff and puff and told

Connor O'Reilly to fetch Mr Potter
the Caretaker because of all the wasps
there wasn't.

Then it was Home Time. Mrs Mullet
never finished the story so I still don't
know what happened to the gingerbread
man, so I asked Lucian Lovejoy and he
said, 'The gingerbread man just went
stale because he wasn't a real man, he
was a biscuit.'

Only, he wasn't sure because he wasn't
listening either.

So I asked Ben Silverstein, who is in
my class and knows everything, and he
said, 'The gingerbread man was a secret
agent *pretending* to be a gingerbread man
– fact!'

But Saloni Doshi, who is also in my

class, said, 'Do
not listen to
him, Delilah.
I'm telling
you that the
gingerbread
man was eaten
by a big bad wolf.'

So I still didn't know for certain and nor did anybody else, so Mrs Mullet went grumble, grumble, groan and gave everybody the story of the gingerbread man to take home.

'Ask your parents or carers to read it to you at the weekend,' she said. 'On Monday, I will choose somebody who's been listening nicely to be the gingerbread man in our play.'

'I've been listening nicely, Mrs Mullet,' said Horrid Charlotte.

'Listen to this,' said Ben Silverstein. 'The part's mine. The play is called The Gingerbread *Man*, not The Gingerbread Silly Little Girl.'

But Mrs Mullet said, 'No name-calling, please. The gingerbread man doesn't have to be a boy. I will be choosing someone who can sit up beautifully and doesn't keep shouting out.'

'I never shout out,' shouted Lucian Lovejoy.

And guess what Horrid Charlotte did? She sat up on purpose in what she thought was a beautiful way and Mrs Mullet said, 'See how nicely Charlotte is sitting, everybody?'

I bet Horrid Charlotte gets to be the gingerbread man. She always gets the best parts in the school plays because she's such a show-off. Maybe if I learn all the gingerbread man's words off by heart by Monday, Mrs Mullet will see what a good actress I am and she'll choose me to be the gingerbread man. Charlotte

Griggs can be the old witch or something.

I need to start practising, which is why Gigi has to get off the phone right now and read me *The Gingerbread Man*.

Which is why I've just pretended to her that Smallboy is playing with scissors.

Chapter Two

At last, Gigi has read me the play about the gingerbread man. It is quite good, but he has to do an awful lot of running. This is because everyone wants to eat him: the old lady who baked him, the old man, and even the cow and the horse and the pig.

Then, when he's trying to cross the

river, the fox tricks him, which I don't think is very nice. The fox tells the gingerbread man he will carry him to safety, but he's fibbing. He tells him to jump on to his tail, then his back, then his nose, but then, guess what? The fox gobbles him all up and that's the end of the story. I feel very sorry for the gingerbread man actually.

Gigi doesn't feel sorry for him one little bit. She says, 'Delilah, darling, this Monsieur Gingerbread? He has the raisins for eyes and the buttons of chocolate all down his front. He is asking to be eaten. It is how he wanted to go, *non*?'

No, it wasn't! If the gingerbread man wanted to be eaten, he'd have stood still!

In the land where I come from, gingerbread men never get eaten. They meet a nice gingerbread lady and they have gingerbread babies and they all live happily ever after in a gingerbread house. Or if they are very old like my nana and grandpa and have wobbly legs, they live in a gingerbread bungalow, which is a house with no upstairs.

'Don't they ever be eating of biscuits in your Far Away Land?' Gigi asks. Well, of course they do! But not if the biscuits have faces and not if they talk.

My mother has just come home from work. She is an Inferior Designer. An Inferior Designer is someone who goes round to people's houses and tells them that their curtains don't match the rug and to get rid of their nasty wallpaper and that they mustn't put paper clips and hairbands in the fruit bowl.

Sometimes she comes into my own bedroom and tries to do Inferior Designing. She says, 'Delilah, darling, your room is such a mess. Those knickers and dinosaurs shouldn't be on the floor and why is there half a bowl of strawberry jelly on your pillow?'

So I say, 'But everyone has a bowl of

strawberry jelly on their pillow in the land where I come from,' and she says, 'Let's not go there, shall we?' and runs around making everything horribly tidy.

When she comes home, I run all the way down the stairs and I shout, 'Run, run as fast as you can!' and my mother looks really scared and says, 'Should I? Why? Is there a fire?'

I do wish she'd let me finish explaining, so I say, 'Run, run as fast as you can, you can't catch me, because I'm the bread man!'

I forgot to say ginger. It's *ginger*bread man. Gingerbread man. I must remember the right words or Mrs Mullet will make me be the cow or the horse or the pig instead.

'I'm practising for the school play,' I tell her.

'How lovely,' she says. 'You were such a good tree in *Little Red Riding Hood*.'

It wasn't even a speaking tree, but she says, 'Never mind, darling. You waved beautifully in the breeze. You were the best tree in the forest. Everybody said so, Delilah.'

'But I didn't want to be a tree! I wanted to be the big bad wolf, but Horrid Charlotte Griggs got the part and she can't even growl.'

The only reason she got to be the wolf was because her uncle owns a shop in Wincey Road which sells material, and Charlotte told Mrs Mullet that if she let her be the big bad wolf, her

mother would sew her the best costume
ever because she can get as much free
fur fabric as she wants. And stuffing
and glass eyes.

I really, really want to be the
gingerbread man. My mother knows
she has to practise my lines with me, but
I'm afraid she'll try and escape to do
something she really enjoys like cleaning
the oven, so I fall down on the rug and I
wail, 'You have to help me or I will *die*.'

'What a good actress you are,' she says.
'I will do it as soon as I have fed Arnold
and Ambrose.'

In case you don't
know, Arnold is my
dog and Ambrose is
my cat. After they've

had their dinner, I sit in the fat armchair with my mother, who pretends to be everyone who isn't the gingerbread man. She isn't very good at acting though, so I have to point out her mistakes.

'You just went *Neighhh* when you were meant to go *Moooo*.'

'I'm terribly sorry, Delilah, darling.'

I tell her not to worry. Where I come from, there is a sort of cow that sounds just like a horse.

'I'm so glad to hear it,' she says. 'Now I don't feel nearly as silly.'

Then Daddy comes home, so I say to him, 'You're a pig and you have to chase me so I can practise running as fast as I can.'

'Why must I?' he says. 'I am rather tired, Delilah.'

He's tired? Well, that's funny because I'm a bit tired of having to explain everything.

'I'm the *gingerbread* man.'

'Oh,' he says. 'I know that story. Can't I be the fox instead? Climb on my back.'

So I do and he runs round and round the house and up the stairs.

He's marbellous for his age, but my
mother tells him to stop it because
Arnold is going bark, bark bark because
he likes chasing us so much.

At bedtime, my mother says, 'Delilah,
darling, please don't be too disappointed
if you don't get the part. There are lots of
other children in the class, remember.'

I tell her that they don't stand a
chance.

'I run like a gingerbread man. I talk
like a gingerbread man. I even look like
a gingerbread man in my ginger tights
with this cushion stuffed up my ginger
jumper, don't I?'

'You do look a picture,' she says, 'but I
think it would be best if you didn't wear
that costume in bed, Delilah. Change

into your pyjamas or you will bake.'

The little old lady put the gingerbread man in the oven to bake. But he jumped up and ran right out of the cottage, shouting, 'Don't eat me!'

See? I know all the words. But I bet Charlotte Griggs comes to school on Monday dressed in the best gingerbread man costume ever, made from free ginger material.

In the land where I come from, it is very rude to turn up in a better costume than the queen, but I'm afraid that's Horrid Charlotte Griggs all over.

Chapter Three

It's Monday morning and Gigi has just walked me all the way to my school, which is called Wheatfields Infants. Smallboy is sitting in his pushchair and singing a funny song about A Rice Pudding Shark in Far Away Language. Only, I'm not laughing because I'm in a rather bad mood.

I am extremely cross with my mother because she would not let me wear my very good gingerbread man costume to school. She made me take off my ginger tights, my ginger hat and the ginger jumper with the cushion stuffed up it. I have to wear my boring grey and red uniform and when I asked why, she said, 'It's the school rule.'

I think it's a very silly rule actually. In the land where I come from, you don't have to wear a school uniform. You can wear any fancy costume you like. You can dress up as a fairy or a peapod or a spaceman if you want. You can even go as a pantomime donkey if you have a friend who doesn't mind being the tail end.

I said to my mother, 'I bet Charlotte Griggs's mother lets her come to school dressed as a gingerbread man.'

But all she said to that was, 'Well, I'm not Charlotte Griggs's mother.'

And then she said, 'What is that stuck to your chin? Oh, it's a cornflake.' And then she scrubbed it off very hard with a flannel and said, 'Now off you go, Delilah, darling. Be a good girl. Good luck with the audition!'

In case you don't know, an audition is when Mrs Mullet decides if it will be me or Horrid Charlotte Griggs who gets the best part in the play.

At the school gates, I wave goodbye to Gigi and Smallboy. Smallboy looks up at me and he says, 'Deedee, you are the best

actress in the universe. If you do not get
to be the gingerbread man, there is no
Justins in this world.' At least, I think
that's what he said. It was in Far Away
Language and he has got a bit of a cold.

'*Bonne chance*, Delilah!' says Gigi,
which is French for There's a good
chance you'll get to be the bun, Delilah.
When she said bun, I think she meant
gingerbread man because he is a sort of
bun, but she's not very good at talking
English, I'm afraid. It's just as well I'm
good at French!

I go into the playground and I sit on
the bench by the drinking fountain.
While I'm studying my play, my best
friend Edie Chadwick, who lives on the
corner of my road which is Sherwood

Avenue, sits next to me and she says, 'I wonder what Horrid Charlotte Griggs has got in that big round tin. Do you wonder, Delilah?'

Charlotte Griggs has already lined up to go into the classroom and Mrs Mullet hasn't even rung the bell yet. I don't care what's in her tin though, because hooray, hooray she isn't dressed as a gingerbread man. Not even a little bit. She has her school uniform on the same as me. Maybe she's not so horrid after all. Although she is wearing very horrid shoes.

'I want to know what's in that tin,' says Edie. 'I bet it's Trouble.'

So she lines up behind Charlotte Griggs and taps her on the shoulder and

says, 'What have you got in that tin,
then?' And Charlotte pulls her best
horrid face and says, 'I'm not telling you,
Edie Chadwick. It's a secret.'

So we all start guessing and Edie says
is it sweets? And Charlotte says no, it isn't
sweets, so there! Then Ben Silverstein
says is it rocking-horse poop? And she
says no, it isn't rocking-horse poop,

actually. You don't know everything, Ben, so ha-dee-ha. Then Lucian Lovejoy says is it a badger? And she says no, why would I bring a badger to school, you silly, silly little boy.

So I tell her that where I come from, we always celebrate National Badger Day at school on this day of the year. It's the rules. Everyone has to dress in black and white, which is badger colours, and we all go to the forest and get on our hands and knees and do the Badger Dance.

'Why?' asks Charlotte.

'Because that's what we do.'

'Oh, do you really, Delilah?' says Charlotte. 'I don't even believe you. How does the Badger Dance go, then?'

So I show her, and everyone in the class joins in with this marbellous dance except for her because she doesn't want to let go of her tin in case we peek.

We're just getting to the bit where we wave our legs in the air and shout 'Badger Ho!' when suddenly Mrs Mullet creeps up and rings her bell very loudly.

'Class Two!' she says. 'What do you think you're doing?'

And Lucian Lovejoy says, 'We're doing the Badger Dance.'

'Well, don't,' says Mrs Mullet. 'I'm glad to see one of you is lining up properly. Well done, Charlotte. The rest of you, stand up. Just look at your knees. That's not how we behave.'

'It *is* where Delilah comes from,' says Lucian.

But before I can explain about National Badger Day, Horrid Charlotte Griggs shakes her tin and says, 'Guess what I've got in here, Mrs Mullet.'

Well, Mrs Mullet looks ever so interested because Charlotte Griggs is always buying her presents, and she says, 'Ooh, has your mother baked another lovely carrot cake for the school bizarre?'

'No, it's not cake,' says Charlotte. 'It's much cleverer than cake.'

'It's not a badger either, Mrs Mullet,' says Lucian helpfully.

Charlotte opens the tin and Mrs Mullet says, 'How wonderful, Charlotte. How clever. Are they all for us?'

'There's one each,' says Charlotte. 'And they're nut-free so even fussy children with allergies can have one. Mummy baked them in case I burned myself, but that's all she did. I did all the hard work. I rolled out the dough and I put the raisins and the buttons on specially all by myself. The biggest one is for you, Mrs Mullet.'

Raisins? Buttons? Oh no. Guess what's in the tin. It's gingerbread men!

'Isn't that kind?' says Mrs Mullet. 'Perhaps we can all have one after lunch. Let's say thank you to Charlotte, everybody.'

I'm thinking, 'Thanks for nothing, Charlotte Griggs.' You know what's going to happen now, don't you? She'll get to be the gingerbread man for being Teacher's Pet and I'll be the wooden spoon or something.

Chapter Four

We have been doing auditions for our school play called *The Gingerbread Man* all morning. We were in the hall, but now we are back in our classroom and Mrs Mullet says we are being too noisy. I don't think we are, but she says we must be quiet or she won't tell us who she has chosen to be who.

'Be quiet, everybody!' shouts Charlotte Griggs.

'Be quiet yourself!' shouts Edie Chadwick.

Then Mrs Mullet says we must all put our fingers on our lips and not say a single word or scrape our chairs, or we won't be able to hear what she has to say.

I think I might have got the part I want after all. I deserve it. Earlier, when we were in the hall, everyone who wanted to be the Gingerbread Man had to put their hands up. My best boyfriend Lucian Lovejoy put his hand up, but he was told to put it down because he kept shouting 'Ginger Nuts!' and making his shoes squeak.

Of course, Horrid Charlotte put her

hand up. And me and everyone else except for Saloni Doshi. When Mrs Mullet asked Saloni Doshi why she didn't want to be the gingerbread man, she said she wanted to be Little Red Riding Hood instead.

'But Little Red Riding Hood isn't in this play,' said Mrs Mullet.

We did *Little Red Riding Hood* last year. Saloni got her plays muddled up, and when Mrs Mullet told her, she cried so hard that she snorted stuff out of her nose.

When she'd finished snorting, everyone in the class who wanted to be the gingerbread man had to go up on to the stage and say the words and do the actions. Some people were a bit shy and just stood there. Some people couldn't remember the words and some people were too quiet, like Rupert Sinclair-Smythe. When Mrs Mullet asked Rupert to speak up, he said he would in a minute, but Mrs Mullet said there wasn't a minute to spare so he didn't bother.

But I was extremely good. Lucian Lovejoy clapped and whooped for ages and ages until Mrs Mullet asked him to be quiet, so he clapped and whooped quietly. Then she said please stop it altogether, Lucian, or nobody will be able to hear Charlotte saying her lines.

Well, I thought Charlotte Griggs was a bit rubbish and so did Edie Chadwick. Edie said Charlotte's voice didn't sound *biscuity* enough for a start. And she wasn't

running nearly fast enough for a
gingerbread man, so we all shouted,
'Run, run as fast as you can!'

And Charlotte pulled a face and said,
'I'm doing it the *ballet* way. I'm in Grade
Three, you know.'

Then she went leap and twirl and leap
and she said, 'You can't catch me, I'm the
– Agghhhh!'

This is because she caught her silly shoe in her silly skirt and fell over. She wasn't hurt a bit and we didn't mean to giggle, but we couldn't help it. Her skirt went right over her head and we all saw her pink pants with teddies on.

We kept giggling and giggling until just now because Mrs Mullet is about to choose who is going to be the gingerbread man. Lucian Lovejoy says it should be me because I did the best running and Edie Chadwick says it should be me because I never got a single word wrong and I didn't mumble and I didn't trip and I'm her best friend.

'It'll be you!' she says.

Mrs Mullet says, 'It's going to be . . .

it's going to be . . . Charlotte Griggs.'

I don't believe it. Everyone else goes 'O . . . oh!' because they're really disappointed, except for Charlotte, who just does her best horrid grin and says, 'Thank you, Mrs Mullet. I always try and do my best, don't I?'

It is not fair. Mrs Mullet says it wasn't because Charlotte was the best – we were all very good, but she's giving her the part because she didn't cry when she had that little fall.

'I can have a little fall and not cry,' I tell her.

'So can I!' says Edie Chadwick.

'So can I,' says Lucian Lovejoy. 'I can have a *big* fall. I could jump off this chair and bang my head on that cupboard and not even cry. I'll show you, shall I?'

But Mrs Mullet says, 'No thank you. Get down please, Lucian. We don't want any more accidents. Let's all sit quietly on our chairs.'

'I'm sitting quietly!' yells Horrid Charlotte Griggs.

Then Saloni starts crying again and Mrs Mullet says, 'No, Saloni. I'm afraid you can't be Little Red Riding Hood. She is not in this play, dear. How many more times?'

But that's not why Saloni's crying; she's crying because she's got her finger stuck in her pencil sharpener.

Mrs Mullet has taken Saloni to the school nurse, so now we have to wait even longer to see who we're all going to be. I know I can't be the gingerbread man any more and I don't want to be the pig or the horse or the cow.

'Charlotte Griggs should have been the cow,' says Edie Chadwick.

That's why she's my best friend.

Chapter Five

It is the afternoon. I am still at school and I can now tell you who I am not going to be in the play. I am *not* the Little Old Lady. Which is good because I'm not old and I am not a lady, I'm a queen.

The person who is going to be the old lady is Saloni Doshi. Charlotte

Griggs said, 'But, Mrs Mullet, I don't think Saloni's sensible enough to be the old lady. She'll burn herself on the oven when she bakes the gingerbread man. She can't even be trusted with a pencil sharpener.'

Mrs Mullet said not to worry, it wouldn't be a real oven. It would be a pretend oven and everyone said, a *pretend* oven? You can't cook with a pretend oven!

'Ugh. The gingerbread man will be raw,' said Edie Chadwick.

'You can't eat raw cake mixture,' said Lucian Lovejoy and he started making Being Sick noises until Mrs Mullet told him not to be so unpleasant.

'But that's what'll happen,' he said.

'It'll be germy if it's not cooked.'

But Mrs Mullet said to stop swinging on his chair and being silly. Everyone uses pretend objects in a play, she said. They are what we call props. After all, the gingerbread man has to get across the river and we couldn't have a real river in the school hall, now could we?

'Why not?' I say. 'In the land where I come from, everyone has a real river in the school hall. On hot days, we wear our swimming costumes and we paddle in it and sometimes we fish for tadpoodles, which are like tadpoles only they turn into dogs instead of frogs. Then in the winter, when the river freezes, we all do ice skating.'

'Excuse me, Delilah, I was talking,' says Mrs Mullet. 'We are having a pretend river made from a big blue silky sheet and it'll be lovely.'

'Mrs Mullet, how will a sheet look like a river?' asks Charlotte Griggs. 'Only, I need to know because I'm the gingerbread man. Will it be a wet sheet?'

Lucian Lovejoy starts snorting and snorting because he thinks wet sheets are ever so funny and he snorts so loudly that Mrs Mullet says, 'Well, I think

Lucian Lovejoy had better be the pig in our play. Would you like to be the pig, Lucian?' and he goes snort, snort, snort.

SNORT SNORT SNORT

So that's how he got the part. But if he's silly or if he fidgets or if he continues to call out in the classroom, he will not be allowed to be the pig. Someone else who knows how to behave will be the pig and Lucian will have to wave the end of the blue silky sheet with Darren Paisley and Rupert Sinclair-Smythe instead.

After that, Lucian Lovejoy is awfully good and quiet because he so wants to be the pig. Mrs Mullet has chosen Ben Silverstein to be the little old man. This is because he's got the loudest voice. She asked Edie Chadwick to be the front of the horse, but when Edie heard that Connor O'Reilly was going to be the back end, she asked to be the cow instead. She was worried Connor might kick her in the bottom because that's what he does.

Mrs Mullet said everyone else could be the Narrators, which is the people who say the story and hold up pictures because they can't act. I was thinking, oh that's it then, and feeling fed up because I should have been the gingerbread man. I really should. Lucian is being no fun either because he's behaving, and I don't even want to do this silly play, when suddenly Mrs Mullet says, 'Oops, I forgot the fox, didn't I?'

Straight away, Lucian Lovejoy puts his hand up and he says, 'Delilah Darling should be the fox because of her badger dance, Mrs Mullet.'

'Yes, Delilah should be the fox,' says Edie Chadwick.

'Oh, honestly!' says Horrid Charlotte. 'Just because Delilah Darling can do a badger dance doesn't mean she'll be any good as a fox. There isn't a fox dance in the play. Foxes and badgers aren't even the same anyhow, are they, Mrs Mullet? Foxes are mammals and badgers are reptiles.'

'Actually,' says Mrs Mullet, 'they are both mammals.'

'Correct!' says Ben Silverstein.

'I'm good at mammals,' I tell her. 'In the land where I come from, whenever there was a school play, I was always the mammal.'

'No you weren't,' says Charlotte. 'You're just making it up.'

Lucian Lovejoy goes *herumph* and then he puts his hand up again, very politely so he can still be the pig, and Mrs Mullet says, 'What is it now, Lucian?' and he says, 'Mrs Mullet, I just want to say that Delilah really was a mammal in a play in the Land Where She Comes From. She was a furry mammal with four legs and a tail called a ... what was it called, Delilah?'

'A Golden Mungming,' I remind him.

'Oh yes. It was a Golden Mungming, Mrs Mullet,' he says. 'I saw Delilah being a Mungming and it was just like the real thing. I clapped really, really loudly.'

'Yes, well you would, wouldn't you, Lucian?' says Mrs Mullet.

I think she must have believed him though because, guess what? I got the part! I'm going to be the fox in the school play. I didn't really want to be the fox at first, but it's better than being the river or the spoon. I shall be a very good fox. I will be even more brilliant as a fox than a Mungming. Tonight I shall practise prowling and howling in the garden.

And best of best, at the end of the play, because I'm the fox, I get to eat the gingerbread man, who is Horrid Charlotte Griggs.

How everyone will cheer.

Chapter Six

When I get home from school, I tell my mother I am going to be the fox and she says, 'Delilah, darling, that's wonderful. I know you wanted to be the gingerbread man, but actually the fox is the best character because he's the baddy and he is very clever.'

She's right. The gingerbread man isn't

very clever. He can't even swim, you know. I think if he tried, he would go soggy. Or maybe he can swim, but didn't like to because he didn't have a swimming costume. Once I didn't have a swimming costume because it fell out of my towel on the bus on the way to the swimming pool and Gigi said, 'Perhaps you can be swimming in these knicketies of Smallboy's. I think they will be fitting you. They are stretchily.'

But Smallboy yelled, 'No!' in Far Away Language. He stamped his feet and he said, 'My sister is not borrowing my knicketies. They are my special ones with a stegosaurus on.'

At least that's what I think he said, but it was hard to tell because he was

stamping so hard and then he lay on
his back and kicked and screamed. So
I didn't get to swim that day, like the
gingerbread man.

The fox can swim though. I do want
to be the fox, but the trouble is he has
lots of words to say in this play. When he
sees the gingerbread man trying to cross
the pretend river which is really the blue
sheet, he has to say three whole things.

He has to say, 'Jump on my tail,
gingerbread man. I will take you across
the river.' Then he has to say, 'You are
too heavy for my tail. Jump on my back.'
Then he has to say, 'You are too heavy
for my back. Jump on my nose.' Then he
eats him.

Only, I'm a bit scared I'll forget which

way round I'm meant to say it all. I tell my mother this and she says, 'Do not worry, Delilah, darling. You have a whole week to practise.'

But I know what will happen. When I want to practise, she'll be busy. And when she wants to practise, I'll be busy.

'We can practise now, if you like,' she says. But I'm busy. I have to go round to Edie Chadwick's. She has promised we can take her pet guinea pigs out on our scooters. Only, when we get there, her mother who is called Mrs Chadwick says, 'What have you got in that basket, girls?' and Edie says, 'Nothing,' and Mrs Chadwick says, 'Well, I hope it's not guinea pigs. Where are you taking them?'

Edie says, 'Nowhere.' Then her mother

says, 'Edie, you are not to take the guinea
pigs out on your scooters. They are not
toys.' So we have to put them back in
their hutch, which is a shame. In the
land where I come from, we always
give our pets rides on our scooters.
We put them in a basket and hang
the basket on the handle bar
and we go *bobbabobbabobba*
all the way down the
hill and they
don't mind
one little
bit.

'Oh well,' says Edie. 'What shall we do now, Delilah? Shall we look for fairies or shall we tie some meat on a string and post it through Mrs Woolly Hat's letter box?'

Sometimes we do that and we catch a kitten. Mrs Woolly Hat doesn't mind a bit. She likes us ever so much and never tells us off. She is my favourite old person who isn't my nana or grandpa. She lives behind the fence at the bottom of my garden in a big old house and she has cats in all different sizes and colours.

My mother says Mrs Woolly Hat is a Friend Of The Family. She used to take me out in my pram when I was a baby. Before Gigi came, she used to look after me at our house when my mother and father went to a Dinner and Dance or something. It was great fun because she isn't really like a grown-up. She is more like one of us, only wrinkly. She is very interested in the Far Away Land. Sometimes she seems to know more about it than I do. I think she lived there too when she was little.

Mrs Woolly Hat is always putting things through our letter box. Sometimes it's fairy biscuits with icing on top. Sometimes it's very old chocolate fingers, and once it was a cardigan my mother promised to mend – only, Arnold found it first and ate it.

'So what shall we do, Delilah?' asks Edie.

I tell her I should like to go and fish for kittens through Mrs Woolly Hat's letter box. We looked for fairies yesterday but we found so many it got boring. Edie's brother Simon told fibs and said they weren't fairies, they were daddy-long-legs, and he let them out of the jar and they all flew away, so I'm not playing that again.

Anyway, Edie found some string but her mother didn't have any meat to put on the end because she is a vegetarian so then we couldn't think what to do.

'We could tie some coleslaw on the string,' says Edie. 'Do cats like coleslaw, Delilah?'

'No, it's rabbits that like coleslaw and Mrs Woolly Hat doesn't have any rabbits.'

So Edie says, 'Does she have any fizzy drinks? My mother never lets me have fizzy drinks.'

'Why?' I ask her. 'Is it because she's vegetarian?'

And she says, 'No, it's because she's mean.'

When I tell her that Mrs Woolly Hat always gives me fizzy cola with a bendy straw, Edie says, 'My mother never lets me have a bendy straw. Let's go to the bottom of your garden and practise being the fox and the cow really loudly. Then Mrs Woolly Hat will think there are wild animals about and come out of her house to feed them. Then, when she sees it's us, she'll be so pleased, she'll say, "Hello, you two!" and ask us in for some fizzy cola. Isn't that a good idea, Delilah?'

I think it's a brilliant idea. So off we go.

Chapter Seven

Me and Edie have been down the bottom of my garden howling and mooing like a fox and a cow for ages and ages. I'm going *A-rooooooooo!* And Edie is going *Murgggggh!* And Smallboy is going *Nyaaaaaaaah!* because he doesn't want to be left out. Now, for some reason, my mother comes running down the garden, going *Shhhhhhh!*

I tell her she's not meant to be listening and that we are performing for Mrs Woolly Hat. But she says it would be a lot quieter if we knocked on Mrs Woolly Hat's door and asked politely if she would like to hear about our play. And if we were going there, would we please take back the photo album she lent us.

Mrs Woolly Hat's photo album has lots of black-and-white photographs in it because they were taken in the olden days when there were no colours. Only, in the photographs, Mrs Woolly Hat is very young. Gigi said Mrs Woolly Hat was Tray Bell which means she was as beautiful as a tray, in French.

In her best photo,
Mrs Woolly Hat is
wearing a white dress
like a princess and
feathers on her head
like a cockatoo. Over her
shoulder she is wearing what looks like a
squashed cat with long ears and a fat tail
and staring eyes. Only, my mother says,
'That's not a cat, Delilah. It's a fox fur.
All the actresses used to wear them.'

I didn't know Mrs Woolly Hat was an
actress like me, but my mother says, 'Oh
yes! And she was a dancer. She was quite
famous in her day.'

Well, I've never heard of an actress
called Mrs Woolly Hat and neither had
Edie, but my mother says, 'Well, I'm not

surprised. Mrs Woolly Hat isn't her real name, Delilah. That's the name you made up for her when you were little. Her stage name is Ruby Valentine.'

In case you don't know, a stage name is a name you give yourself when you are an actress if your real name is too boring. I know this because Mrs Woolly Hat told me and Edie.

When we went round to see her, we told her we were going to be in a play called *The Gingerbread Man*. She said, 'How divine. But if you are to be actresses, you must change your names to something more glamorous. You, Delilah! Your stage name will be Delicious Dumpling, and you, Edie Chadwick? You are Ida Charming.'

Then Mrs Woolly Hat who is really Ruby Valentine gave us both cola with a bendy straw and cat hairs and Ida Charming said, 'Why isn't it fizzy, Delilah?'

And I said, 'It's Delicious.'

And she said, 'No it isn't, it tastes nasty.'

So I said, 'I wasn't talking about the drink, I was talking about me. I am Delicious. I'm Delicious Dumpling and you're Ida Charming. Those are our stage names.'

'Yes, but why isn't this cola fizzy?' she said.

I told her that's how actresses drink it. In the land where I come from, the actresses never drink fizzy drinks in case it makes them burp when they're on stage. It's the bubbles that do it. If you don't believe me, ask Lucian Lovejoy. He's very windy.

'So what are your roles?' asked Mrs Woolly Hat.

'I'll have cheese in mine, please,' said Ida Charming.

I said I'd have ham, but Mrs Woolly Hat said she wasn't talking about bread rolls, which was a shame because we were both starving.

'When I said what are your roles, I meant which parts are you going to play?' said Mrs Woolly Hat.

'I'm a cow,' said Edie-Ida.

'Ah, but what sort of cow?' asked Mrs Woolly Hat. 'Is it a moody cow? Is it a mad cow? Is it a happy cow? To play the part, you have to know the character inside out.'

Edie thought and thought and then she said, 'It's a hungry cow.'

'It's mad with hunger,' said Mrs Woolly Hat. 'How do we know this? Because it wants to eat ginger and cows are meant to eat grass.'

Then she charged round her front room like a mad cow to show Edie how to do it.

'I'm the fox,' I told her.

'A fox?' said Mrs Woolly Hat. 'I have the perfect costume.'

She went upstairs and when she came back she had the fox fur on over her shoulder – the one she'd worn in her best black-and-white photo. Only this one was brown.

'I wore this when I played Lady Bracknell in the theatre,' she said. 'Do you know Lady Bracknell at all?'

'Is she the lady who works in the Post Office?' asked Edie. 'The one with the moustache?'

Mrs Woolly Hat said no, that was Mrs Bucknell. Not the same person at all. Then she took the fox fur off and gave it to me and said, 'Try it on, Delicious

Dumpling. It's rather moth-eaten but no matter. No one will notice a little thing like that if you give a grand performance.'

It fitted perfectly. Of course, when Edie saw how much like a real fox I looked with the fox fur hanging down over my face, she wanted a costume that made her look

like a real cow. So she asked Mrs Woolly Hat if she had any udders.

'Udders?' said Mrs Woolly Hat. 'Let me see.'

Well, she looked, but I'm afraid she couldn't find any. Which was a shame because Edie said her mother wouldn't be any good at making a cow costume.

'Is it because she's a vegetarian?' I asked.

But she said, 'No, Delilah. It is because she can't sew for toffee.'

Chapter Eight

We are going to do our school play called *The Gingerbread Man* on Friday. I'm a bit worried because I thought Friday was tomorrow, but Gigi says, 'No, Delilah, darling. Tomorrow is not Friday, it is Sirs Day.'

She cannot say Thursday because she is French and I think they do not have

Thursdays in France. That is a shame because that means they have one less day than us.

In the land far, far away where I come from, we have different days of the week to the ones here. And we have more of them. We have eight whole days. We have Funday, Food Day, Friendsday, Thirstday, Flyday, Happyday, Sunnyday and Myday. It's much better that way.

I wish we had eight days in this land, then my mother would have more time to make me a new fox costume. The reason I need a new one is because yesterday Mrs Woolly Hat's fox fur got awfully torn. It wasn't my fault. All I was doing was seeing what it looked like in front of my mother's long mirror.

When I brought the fox fur home, I showed it to my mother straight away and I thought she'd be pleased and say how marbellous. But she didn't. She said, 'Delilah, darling, it's very sweet of Mrs Woolly Hat to lend you that, but I think I'd better make you a proper costume.'

So I said, 'She hasn't *lent* it to me, she's given it to me for keeps. It's rather lovely, don't you think? I will look just like the best fox.'

My mother just sighed and said, 'Oh dear.'

Then Gigi came into the kitchen holding her nose and she said, '*Quelle horreur!* What is smelling like a fox?'

And my mother pointed to Mrs Woolly Hat's furry thing and said, 'I think it might be best if we put it in the shed.'

Well, I couldn't smell it. And it wasn't nearly as full of holes as people said. And it didn't matter if it only had one glass eye – the fox just looked like it was winking. Which is why I got it out of the shed and took it upstairs and pinned it under my chin with a brooch.

I did this in my mother's room because that was where the brooch was, which needed borrowing. And it was where the mirror was. And it was where Arnold was.

Now, I am allowed in my mother's room if I knock and she says, 'Come in, Delilah,' so I knocked, but she didn't say, 'Come in,' because she wasn't in there.

But she didn't say, '*Don't* come in.' So that is why I went in.

Arnold is not allowed in my mother's room because he steals socks and pants from the linen basket. And he gets doggy paws on the pillows. And he makes puddles.

I didn't let Arnold in, I promise. I didn't even know he was there, really I didn't. He was hiding under the bed on purpose. All I was doing was walking up and down in front of the mirror in the fox fur saying the words in my play. I was pretending to talk to the gingerbread man, only, when I said, 'Jump on to my tail!' Arnold thought I was talking to him.

He jumped on to Mrs Woolly Hat's fox fur tail and he hung on and clung on

even when I spun round and round and he went *grrrrrr, grrrrrrrrr* and the brooch undid and the fox fur fell off and he dragged it under my mother's bed.

He was so pleased with himself, he wouldn't come out. Not until he'd eaten most of it anyway. And he swallowed the glass eye. I thought my mother would be very furious with him but she just said, 'Poor little Arnold, I hope he isn't sick.'

She never said, 'Poor little Delilah.' No. She said, 'I thought Daddy had put that thing in the shed.' And, 'Please ask before you borrow my things.'

She's trying to make me a costume now. She has made a fox mask out of an orange towel stuck to some cardboard. It has whiskers which are really bristles snipped off a broom. The nose is made from a ping-pong ball painted black and there is a piece of elastic at the back to keep the mask on. I don't like the elastic. It keeps getting tangled in my hair and it gives me a headache and I have to tell

my mother this sixty times before she even loosens it.

She says I am giving *her* a headache, but really I'm only trying to help. Sometimes she is quite impossible. She is making me wear Daddy's old brown fishing jumper, which is very itchy. It's too big, so she's pinning it and pinning me and she keeps saying, 'Delilah, darling, stand still!' but I can't stand still because I never do.

She has made the fox tail out of a feather duster but it doesn't look a bit like fur. It looks like something stuck to a chicken's bottom. And now Ambrose is digging his claws right in and trying to eat the feathers because he loves chicken.

Gigi comes in and she says, 'Oh, say mannyfeek Mad Dame!' which means 'I say, that doesn't look anything like a fox' in French.

Then Smallboy says, 'Why is Deedee dressed up as an owl?' in Far Away Language.

Then Daddy comes home and says how clever my mother is to have made me such a brilliant cat costume.

If my own father doesn't even recognize me, goodness knows what Horrid Charlotte Griggs will think I look like.

I am really not looking forward to the dress rehearsal tomorrow.

Chapter Nine

Today is our dress rehearsal for my school play called *The Gingerbread Man*. In case you don't know, a dress rehearsal is where everyone dresses up in their costumes and we all stand on the stage and get our lines wrong.

I didn't think the costume my mother made for me was very brilliant but it's a

lot better than my best friend Edie
Chadwick's. She showed me hers in the
girls' toilets.

'Told you my mum can't sew!' she
said. 'The horns are
wonky and one of
my udders has gone
down.' The udders
were made from
a pink rubber
washing-up
glove. It had
been blowed up

like a balloon and tied with string so the
air couldn't get out. Only, it could
because there was a hole in the thumb.

'Never mind,' I said. 'The show must
go on!' That is what Mrs Woolly Hat

told us. She said if anything ever went wrong with your costume or someone fell over on the stage or your knicker elastic went ping, you just had to act like normal until the play was over. The show must go on, she said.

Mrs Woolly Hat was right actually. Our dress rehearsal went on and on and on and on. We all had to change into our costumes in the classroom except for Horrid Charlotte Griggs, who had been wearing hers since breakfast time. It wasn't made of pretend fur from her uncle's fabric shop though. She'd made her mother knit her a whole gingerbread man costume with knitting needles and wool. It even does up with Velcro at the back because

Charlotte said buttons were too fiddly.

Then, because she wanted to wear her costume to school, she made her mother take her in the car even though she lives right next to Wheatfields Infants. She said she had to have a lift because she couldn't see through the eyeholes properly and might get run over. She wouldn't get run over, I'm afraid, because the lollipop man won't let cars go anywhere near us. He frightens them off with his massive lollipop. Even so, she still got a lift because her mother is so kind and loving.

My mother never gives me a lift. She always makes me walk with Gigi and Smallboy, even when it's raining. I told her that in the land where I come from, the mothers always give their children a lift to school when it's raining and even when it's sunning, but she said, 'It's only drizzling, Delilah. Walking is good for you. Take your pussycat umbrella.'

I took my pussycat umbrella and, actually, it was quite fun because when I got to school, I hooked my umbrella handle in the belt of Lucian Lovejoy's raincoat and he pretended to be a runaway horse and he galloped round and round the playground until his belt broke.

I must say he looks very handsome in his pig costume. Very pink and shiny. The tail on my fox costume has gone a bit soggy because it fell out of my bag into a puddle, but Lucian said it was a good thing. He said it made it more realistic.

'Foxes do like to roll in mud,' he said.

'I think that's pigs,' I told him.

And Lucian said, 'Oh yes. You are right, Delilah. It's pigs that like to roll in mud. I will remember that.'

He did too, because after Mrs Mullet helped him into his costume, she asked him to fetch the register from the school office. In case you don't know, a register is a book with everyone's name in, and when the teacher calls your name out, you have to say, 'Here, Mrs Mullet.' That way, she knows that you are there and haven't run away to join the circus or something.

Only, when she called out Edie's name, Edie didn't answer. So Mrs Mullet said, 'Edie Chadwick?' three times and still Edie didn't answer, even though she was sitting right there in her cow costume.

And when Mrs Mullet said, 'Edie, why aren't you answering?' she said, 'Because my name isn't Edie. My name is Ida Charming.'

Charlotte Griggs said, 'Oh no it isn't.'

But I said, 'Oh yes it is. And my name is Delicious Dumpling, and if you don't believe us, ask Mrs Woolly Hat.'

'Mrs Woolly Hat?' she said. 'What kind of a silly name is that?'

Just as I was about to explain all about stage names and how Mrs Woolly Hat is really called Ruby Valentine, Lucian Lovejoy came back with the register. Only he was covered in mud. All over. He was absolutely filthy muddy and he looked so handsome.

'Good heavens, Lucian,' said Mrs Mullet. 'Did you slip in the playground?'

'I rolled!' he said. 'In a big puddle. Pigs do like mud. Delilah Darling told me.'

'Delilah Dumpling is such a nuisance,' said Horrid Charlotte.

'I'm *Delicious*,' I told her.

'There are days,' sighed Mrs Mullet, 'when I wish I'd stayed in bed.'

After she'd dried Lucian Lovejoy with paper towels, she made us all line up and go into the hall to rehearse our play in our costumes. She said everything had to be perfect for tomorrow.

Tomorrow, all the mums and dads and nanas and grandpas will be coming to watch us. And Gigi and Smallboy and Mrs Woolly Hat.

I just can't wait.

Chapter Ten

Here we all are in the hall having our dress rehearsal for our play called *The Gingerbread Man*. The whole of Class Two are on the stage, only, it's not a very big stage, so there's not much room really.

All the children who are the Narrators who tell the story are standing at the side of the stage on boxes. In the middle of the stage is the pretend oven. It is a toy one that Mrs Mullet borrowed from Reception Class. It has a door that opens so you could put something in, like a jelly, and pretend to cook it. Only, if Charlotte Griggs is the gingerbread man I can't see how she's going to fit in the oven and nor can Lucian.

He puts his hand up and asks, 'Mrs Mullet? Me and Delilah Darling are wondering something.'

'Oh yes,' says Mrs Mullet. 'And what might that be?'

And Lucian says, 'How will the little old lady get Charlotte in the oven because the oven is only little and she's quite chubby?'

'I am *not* chubby,' says Charlotte. 'It's

this costume. The wool is very thick.'

'Even if she is all wool,' says Saloni, 'Charlotte will take a very long time to cook. When my Auntie Priti was cooking a goat for cousin Sindra's wedding it took two whole days and Charlotte Griggs is much fatter than a goat.'

'This is a play,' says Mrs Mullet. 'We are pretending. You are not really going to cook Charlotte, Saloni.'

Saloni looks quite disappointed and she says, 'Then why am I wearing these great big oven mitts?'

Mrs Mullet says, 'Never mind all that. Let's get started or no one will know what they are meant to be doing tomorrow.'

'What are we doing tomorrow?' asks Lucian Lovejoy.

'Our *play*,' says Mrs Mullet. 'Now keep your trotters to yourself, Lucian, and let's begin. Once upon a time, there was a little old lady . . . In you come, Saloni! Pretend to roll the dough. That's right. And you, Ben. Stand next to Saloni. You're meant to be her husband.'

So Saloni rolls the dough and she rolls it and rolls it and everyone's getting really bored, then she pretends to fold the dough into little triangles.

'Use your pastry cutter,' says Mrs

Mullet. 'You are making a gingerbread man.'

But Saloni says, 'No, no, no. I am making Stuffed Samosas because that is what we had at my cousin Sindra's wedding.'

'I should like you to make a gingerbread man,' says Mrs Mullet, 'because that is what our play is about. It is not about your cousin's wedding.'

'Saloni Doshi, you are so annoying,' says Charlotte Griggs, who is hiding behind the curtains waiting to jump out.

'That is because I'm a little old lady,' says Saloni. 'You should respect your elders.'

Mrs Mullet looks at her watch and sighs.

'Can we please get on with it or Class Three will be needing the hall for Music and Movement.'

Finally, Saloni makes a gingerbread man and puts it in the oven with her samosas. Then Charlotte Griggs leaps out from behind the curtain and says, 'Don't eat me!'

'We shan't!' shouts Lucian.

Everyone goes really quiet and Lucian looks worried because if he's naughty

Mrs Mullet won't let him be the pig, but she seems to have forgotten about that.

'Just run,' she says.

So we all start running and two of the Narrators almost fall off their boxes and the horse collapses and Edie Chadwick bursts another udder.

'Stop!' cries Mrs Mullet. 'When I said "Run" I was only talking to the

gingerbread man. Charlotte, say your
line, please, and run away from the little
old lady and the little old man.'

'Shall I do it ballet-style, Mrs Mullet?'

'Just run, dear,' she says. 'Just run.'

So the gingerbread man runs and

then Lucian, who is the pig, is meant to shout, 'Stop, I want to eat you!' Only, he doesn't. He says, 'Run, run as fast as you can, you can't catch me, I'm the gingerbread man.'

'No,' says Mrs Mullet. 'You're *not* the gingerbread man, are you, Lucian? You are the pig. What does the pig say?'

Lucian Lovejoy thinks very hard then he shrugs his shoulders and he shouts, '*Oink! Oink!*'

I don't think it was the right thing to say because Mrs Mullet is pulling a very strange face. Then she gets really cross with Connor O'Reilly. He wants to be the front of the horse and because she's making him be the back end he does a hilarious dance and one of the Narrators

who is called Kyle laughs so hard he
wees and he has to go and borrow some
shorts from the Lost Property Box.

I think this dress rehearsal is going
quite well really. It was a lot worse
when we did *Little Red Riding Hood*
but Mrs Mullet keeps on being a bit
of a misery. She looks really fed up all
the way through this jolly good play
until Edie, who is the cow, comes on.
She says her lines perfectly and she
does really good actions and marbellous
mooing.

'Excellent, Edie.' Mrs Mullet claps.

'Ida,' says Edie.

The reason Edie is so good at being
the cow is because of Mrs Woolly Hat,
of course – she's been teaching us how

to do acting. I can do a really good sly fox now. I can't wait till it's my turn to eat the gingerbread man.

Charlotte Griggs had better watch out because, actually, fox's teeth are quite sharp.

Chapter Eleven

Today is Friday, which means this afternoon is our school play at last. I'm a bit tired though. I went to bed early, but I couldn't sleep because I had a tickly feeling in my tummy. My mother said it was butterflies, which is odd, because I didn't eat any.

I couldn't finish my dinner because I

was so excited, even though it was rabioli, which is my favourite. In case you don't know, rabioli is little squishy parcels with frilly ends. It comes from a town called Italy and it is made of pasta in red sauce which always goes down your shirt.

Once, when Smallboy was even smaller and in his high chair, he had some rabioli. He liked it so much he put his whole face in the bowl, right up to his ears. My mother wasn't very pleased. I told her that in the land where I come from, that is how everyone eats rabioli because it saves washing up the spoons, but she said, 'Well, that is not how we eat it in this house.'

My mother is in a funny mood. I

think she's a bit overexcited about coming to see me in my play. She doesn't get out a lot, poor thing. Gigi is coming too. She is going to the shops this morning to buy a new outfit specially. She has to do that because she is French and she says that she cannot possibly wear old-fashioned clothes like the people of England.

Daddy is coming too. And Nana and Grandpa Darling. Mrs Woolly Hat will be coming, of course. We are only supposed to invite relatives because there aren't enough chairs to go round at Wheatfields Infants. But I asked Mrs Mullet please could Mrs Woolly Hat pretend to be my auntie and she said, 'Oh, all right. Just this once. But don't tell everybody or they'll all want to bring their pretend aunties too and Mr Potter won't be pleased.'

Mr Potter is our school caretaker. A caretaker is someone who throws sawdust on the floor if someone has been sick and puts the chairs out when we do plays. Then afterwards he has to put all the chairs away again. It is quite a fun job if you like chairs.

The only thing I don't like about Mr Potter is that he doesn't care for snow. When it snows, he puts grit on the playground. Me and Lucian Lovejoy don't understand why he does that. We wait all year for it to snow and then, when it does and we run outside to go sliding, we can't go sliding because

Mr Potter has melted the snow on
purpose with his grit which is mean
and wicked of him.

Gigi's taking me to school in a minute. My mother wishes me good luck and says she'll see me at three o'clock because that's when everyone's coming to see the play. I tell her that when she comes to my school she has to wear the clothes I have put out for her. I have to do this otherwise she will turn up in something rather silly and everyone will laugh at her.

'But, Delilah, darling,' she says, 'I'm not sure I should wear my silver ball gown and feather boa to your school play. I'll be a bit overdressed, won't I?'

'Nonsense,' I tell her. 'Where I come from, everyone wears their ball gown and boa to the school play. And their highest sparkly shoes.'

As if I haven't got enough to do without helping my own mother choose the right outfit. Mrs Woolly Hat is the only grown-up I know who wears good clothes. She always wears the same marbellous hat, which is purple and woolly. Sometimes if she is going somewhere special like the dentist she even wears another hat over her woolly hat, which I think is quite stylish.

I often wear my queen crown over my school hat even though my mother tries to stop me . . . Ooh! There's one more thing I have to say to her before I go to school and that is this:

'Mother, if you talk to my friends, you mustn't tell them I'm from here. Because I'm not. I come from a land far, far away, remember?'

'How could I forget?' she says. But she does forget quite a lot actually.

❧ 112 ❧

Gigi takes me to school, but when I'm lining up in the playground, Edie Chadwick says, 'Have you noticed anything, Delicious Dumpling?'

And I say, 'What sort of anything, Ida Charming?'

And she says, 'Well! Have you noticed that Somebody Horrid isn't here?'

She's right, Charlotte Griggs isn't here. Maybe she's late, but Ida Charming says Charlotte Griggs is never, ever late. She always likes to be at the front of the queue when we line up to go into the classroom in the morning so that Mrs Mullet can see how good she is.

'Maybe she's had a terrible accident,' says Lucian Lovejoy. 'Maybe a scary monster came into her bedroom in the

middle of the night and took her to
Monster Land.'

Wouldn't that be a happy day? I do
hope he's right.

Chapter Twelve

Everyone is talking about what has happened to Horrid Charlotte. Lucian Lovejoy has told everyone she's been snatched by a scary monster, but Edie says it's absolutely not true.

'No, Delilah,' she says. 'I heard that Charlotte dropped her Ballet Barbie in the supermarket freezer and when she tried to fish the Barbie out, she fell into

the frozen peas and caught a cold called
Poomoanier.'

But Saloni Doshi said that wasn't true
either. 'Believe me,' she said, 'Charlotte
was walking through the woods near her
granny's and she was eaten by a big bad
wolf.'

Mrs Mullet said none of those stories
were true though,
which was a
shame. She said
Charlotte Griggs
had got
Chicken Pox.
She wasn't
very poorly but
she was covered in
red spots and she

wasn't allowed to come back to school until the scabs fell off. Which means that she can't be the gingerbread man in our play this afternoon.

So then Mrs Mullet surprised me very much by saying, 'Delilah, would you like to be the gingerbread man instead? I know you know all the words.'

Now, a long, long time ago, I did *so* want to be the gingerbread man but now I do not.

I want to be the fox because he's the baddy and it's the best part. Also I do not think the gingerbread man costume would suit me, which is what I told Mrs Mullet.

'It would suit me,' said Lucian Lovejoy. 'I know all the words too.'

He stood up and said all of the words right in front of the whole class, and he was the best gingerbread man ever, but Mrs Mullet didn't seem so sure.

'I thought you wanted to be the pig, Lucian,' she said.

But Lucian said, no, he would like to be the gingerbread man because he was always the pig.

He was a pig when we did our play called *Three Little Pigs* and he was a pig when we did *Noah's Ark* and he was the pig when we did *Tom, the Piper's Son* in assembly.

'I'm fed up with being a pig,' he said.

'That's a shame. You do it so well,' said Mrs Mullet. But everyone said, 'Oh, *go* on, Mrs Mullet. Let Lucian Lovejoy be the gingerbread man. He'll be so funny.'

So Mrs Mullet thought and thought,
then she said, 'If I let you be the
gingerbread man, do you promise to
behave, Lucian?'

Lucian promised.
He crossed his
heart and said he
wouldn't call out
and he wouldn't
play with wasps
or chew chalk or
flick people or do
any of the things
he usually does.

'Very well,' she said.
'You can be the gingerbread man. I'm
sure that'll be . . . lovely.'

I shouted hurrah and Lucian shouted hooray until Mrs Mullet looked at him and said, 'You promised, Lucian.' Then he went very quiet and good again.

But now we don't have a pig. Nobody else really wants to be the pig because Lucian's costume is so muddy from where he rolled in the puddle. The only person who does want to be the pig is Rupert Sinclair-Smythe, who is the smallest boy in the class. Rupert Sinclair-Smythe is so small he can't reach his peg to hang his coat up.

Rupert Sinclair-Smythe has a very small voice too. That is why Mrs Mullet chose him to hold the end of the blue silky sheet which is the pretend river.

That way, he doesn't have to say anything. He just has to wave his arms to make ripples.

'I want to be the pig,' he said, and Mrs Mullet said, 'Pardon, Rupert?' because his voice is so tiny. When Mrs Mullet realized he wanted to be the pig, she asked if he could talk very loudly and clearly so that all the mummies and daddies could hear him at the back of the stage.

Then little Rupert Sinclair-Smythe went YESSSSSS! so loudly we couldn't believe it was him. It was so loud, Lucian fell off his chair. It was a very loud voice for such a little boy, but once he'd shouted once, he couldn't seem to stop. I think he realized what enormous fun it was and how everyone couldn't help listening to him, even with our hands over our ears. He liked that very much so he shouted:

'I CAN TALK VERY LOUDLY, MRS MULLET! THE ONLY REASON I DON'T TALK VERY LOUDLY VERY OFTEN IS BECAUSE I'M BUSY THINKING.'

'Oh,' said Mrs Mullet. 'And what are you busy thinking?'

And Rupert Sinclair-Smythe shouted:

'I AM BUSY THINKING, WHAT IF WE ARE ALL REALLY PUPPETS BEING CONTROLLED BY THE MAN ON THE MOON?'

Mrs Mullet didn't know what to say to that really. None of us did. So she said, 'All right, dear. There's no need to shout.' Then she asked him if he could snort.

Well, he said he could, so she said, 'Thank you, Rupert. It is very kind of you to volunteer. But you will have to miss afternoon playtime so I can pin up the legs on the pig costume. It is rather large for you.'

After playtime, we all have to get into our costumes while Mr Potter puts all the chairs out, plus an extra one for Mrs Woolly Hat. It won't be long now before the audience arrives.

Then the show will begin.

Chapter Thirteen

This is so exciting. The whole of Class Two are on the stage wearing their costumes. Me and Lucian are hiding behind the curtains with Ida Charming and the horse and the pig because it is not our turn to go on yet.

All the mummies and daddies are here. I can see Smallboy sitting on Nana's lap. He is wearing Grandpa's glasses upside down. My mother is sitting next to Gigi. Gigi looks very fashionable indeed, but I'm afraid my mother has let herself down a little. Sadly, she is not wearing her ball gown like she was told. I hope she realizes what a ninny she looks.

'There's Mrs Woolly Hat!' says Edie.

Well, she does look marbellous in her dancing dress and tiara, so we call out, 'Hello, Mrs Woolly Hat,' and we wave.

But Mrs Mullet says, 'Shhh. We are actors and actresses. That's enough waving. Everybody ready?'

Saloni Doshi says she wants to go to the toilet, and when she says that, we all want to go, but Mrs Mullet says it's too late and, anyway, we've all just been. We'll have to hang on unless we're

really desperate because the play's about
to start.

Then she says, 'Excuse me, Connor
O'Reilly, why is the horse crossing its
back legs?'

And Connor says, 'I'm desperate,
Mrs Mullet.'

So we all have to wait for Connor to
climb out of the horse costume and go
to the toilet
before the play
can start.
When he
comes back,
Mrs Mullet
stands in
front of all
the parents

and she says, 'Ladies and gentlemen, Class Two will now perform *The Gingerbread Man*. While it is lovely to see so many baby brothers and sisters, if they start crying, please would you take them out as it puts the children off.'

Smallboy shouts, 'I promise not to cry unless it's rubbish!' in Far Away Language, so Nana shushes him and the hall goes quiet.

The Narrator says, 'This is the story of the gingerbread man.'

Then Saloni Doshi makes the gingerbread dough and puts it in the pretend oven and shuts the door.

Then nothing happens.

'What are we waiting for?' asks Lucian Lovejoy rather loudly.

'You,' whispers Mrs Mullet.

'Oh!' he says. 'I'm the gingerbread man, aren't I?'

Then he jumps out from behind the curtains but he does such a big jump, the Velcro in the back of his costume goes *riiiiiiip* and comes undone.

'Don't eat me,' he says. 'Are my pants showing, Delilah?'

'The show must go on!' I whisper.

So he holds on to his woolly knitted trousers so they don't fall down, and he shouts, 'Run, run as fast as you can, you

can't catch me, I'm the gingerbread man!' Then he races round and round the stage like anything.

'I say,' says Mrs Woolly Hat. 'Look at the little beggar go!'

After that it all went very well.
Nobody could hear the pig though.
I think this was because Rupert Sinclair-
Smythe had forgotten what fun it was to
speak up and had started thinking his
strange thoughts about the man in the
moon again.

It didn't matter one bit though
because the audience were so busy
laughing at Ida Charming's udders,
which were dangling by a thread. Edie
didn't mind at all. She likes to make
people laugh. Mrs Woolly Hat was
laughing her head off and prodding my
mother and saying, 'That Edie
Chadwick, she's a card!' at the top of
her voice.

But the best bit of the whole play was

me. Everybody said so afterwards except for Mrs Mullet, who said, 'Well, Delilah, it was certainly different.' Because what happened was this:

When the gingerbread man couldn't get across the river, I told him to hop on my tail like normal, which he did. Then I told him to hop on my back, which he did. But when he hopped on to my nose, I just couldn't bear to eat him, because he was Lucian. I never liked that bit of the story anyway because I think it's very sad, so I changed it.

I said, 'Don't worry, little gingerbread man. I shan't eat you. Let's get married, shall we?'

'Oh . . . OK,' said Lucian and we held hands in the middle of the stage.

The audience went ever so quiet for some reason, so I said, 'The End!' nice and loudly so that the people at the back could hear. Then I bowed, because Mrs Woolly Hat said you had to bow at the end of the play.

Suddenly, everyone started clapping like anything. Nana and Grandpa were cheering and shouting 'Bravo'. Gigi stood up and said, '*Encore*, Delilah!' which is French for Do It Again, Delilah. Only Mrs Mullet doesn't understand French. She thought *Encore* meant Don't Do It Again because when we tried, she wouldn't let us.

Afterwards the grown-ups went and found Mrs Mullet, who had gone all shy and was hiding in her paper cupboard. They all told her how much they loved our play about the gingerbread man. It was very interesting, they said. It was really marbellous. Well done!

'I particularly liked the ending,' said Mrs Woolly Hat. 'Most unexpected.'

'Indeed,' said Mrs Mullet. 'We have Delilah Darling to thank for that.'

But there is no need to thank me, really there isn't. In the land far, far away where I come from, the plays *always* have happy endings.